Weekly Reader Children's Book Club presents

BEAR CIRCUS

The kangaroo and the real
teddy bear are two animals
who live side by side.

The kangaroo is good at hopping across the land.

William Pène du Bois

BEAR CIRCUS

The Viking Press   *New York*

The real teddy bear climbs
well, straight up and down.
The kangaroo is special, and
the real teddy bear is special.

This is a story about true
friendship.

pour PAUL, ALBERT,
et FRANÇOIS FRATELLINI

Koala Park is a place where real teddy bears live together in gum trees.

They climb up and down all day, and sleep and play. They are born, grow up, and live their whole lives in the trees.

The gum tree makes a perfect house for them, because real teddy bears eat only gum-tree leaves.

No other food is good for them.

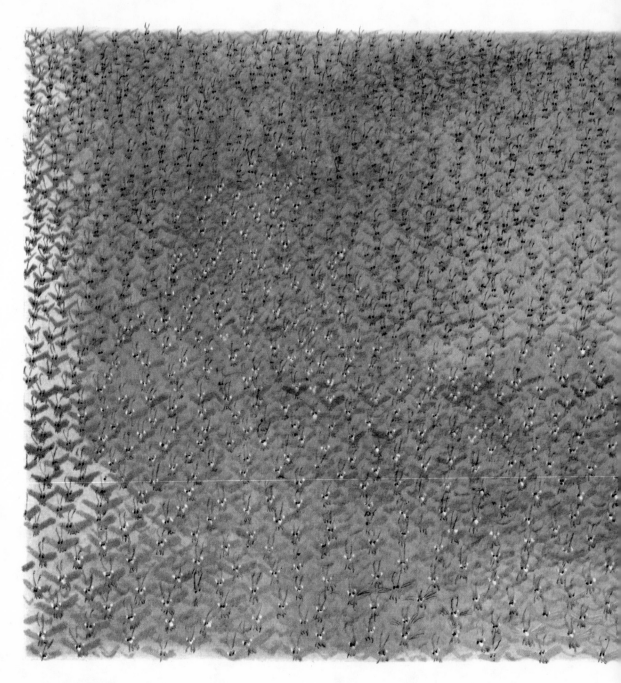

One day a terrible thing happened to the bears of
Koala Park.

It was early morning.

Suddenly a green cloud appeared. It was a thick cloud,
full of tiny eyes, wings, and legs.

The thick cloud was made up of grasshoppers.

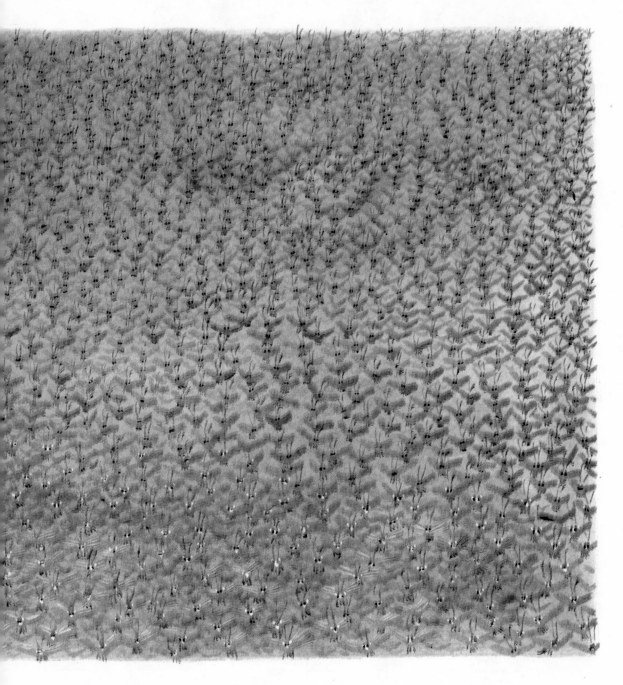

They swooped in over the gum trees. There was a noise like a thousand babies shaking rattles, then, as quickly as they had come, the grasshoppers left.

The bears opened their eyes and looked around them. All their food was gone. The grasshoppers had eaten every leaf off every gum tree.

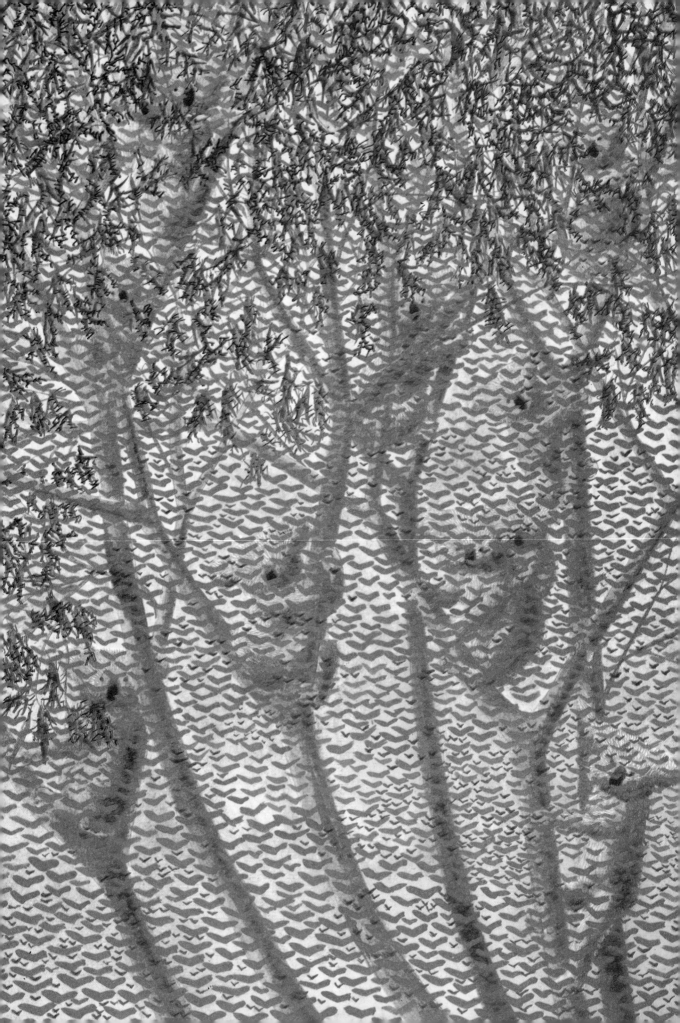

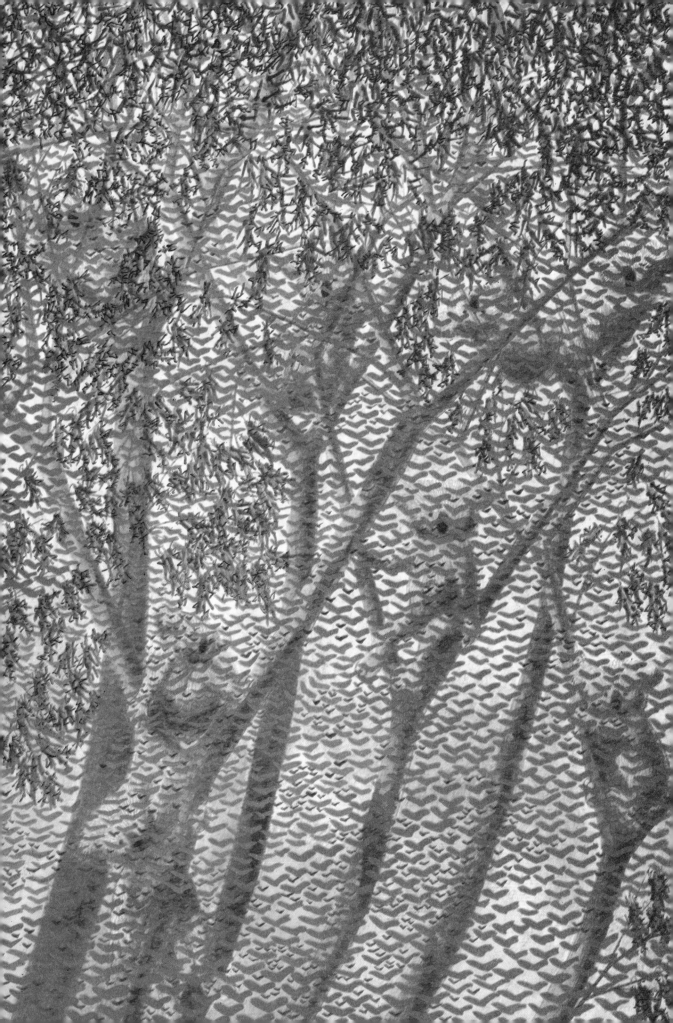

The poor bears were first scared, then sad.

"What will we do now?" they asked each other.

The wise old bear who lived at the top of the tallest gum tree spoke up. "We must leave at once and look for new gum trees," he said, "because every minute spent here will only make us more hungry."

The bears left Koala Park.

Real teddy bears do not walk fast, and the country looked like a desert as far as they could see. Everything green had been eaten by the grasshoppers.

Just as they were thinking they would never eat again there was a loud thumping and bumping sound. The bears turned, and up over the hill hopped their friends the kangaroos.

"Slow down, bears," the kangaroos shouted.

"I guess the grasshoppers stole your food too," said the wise old bear.

"Every last bit of it," said a kangaroo. "May we offer you a ride? We could all look for food together."

"We'd be delighted," said the wise old bear. "What sort of ride had you in mind?"

"Well, some of you might climb into our pockets, and the rest might hang on to our necks. How does that sound?"

"Just fine," said the wise old bear.

"Well, all aboard then," said the kangaroo.

The bears took their places, and the friends were off, thumping and bumping across the countryside.

Now just about the time the bears and the kangaroos were meeting below, a pink airplane was running into the green cloud of grasshoppers above.

The airplane was carrying Colonel Tim's Tiny Time Circus. Each passenger was a little chap, either a dwarf or a midget, and the circus was on a world tour, entertaining children.

The grasshoppers quickly clogged up the airplane's engines, and the airplane started to crash.

"Everybody jump!" the pilot shouted.

There were not enough parachutes to go around, but this didn't bother the little circus men. They all put on a fine show of landing safely.

The pink airplane chugged on quite awhile, all by itself, leaving behind a trail of fried grasshoppers.

IME CIRCUS

With great luck, the bears and the kangaroos soon came across some beautiful gum trees. They were standing straight and were green as a crisp salad. There was a fine beach and the sea behind them.

The crashing pink airplane arrived at the same place at just about the same time.

"What is that?" asked a baby bear.

"I never saw anything like it," said his friend.

The pink airplane crashed into a million tiny bits, scattering pretty circus things all over the bears' new home.

"It must have been a Christmas present which opens itself," said the baby bear.

"I think you are right," said his friend.

The circus things were too small for the kangaroos, and just a little too big for the bears. It was decided that the bears should keep them.

"This is as it should be," said the wise old bear to the kangaroos. "You saved our lives today. We shall put on a circus for you when we are ready. It's the least we can do for you."

"Great idea," said the kangaroos. "Now we must go and look for our own food."

The friends said good-by, and the bears climbed into their new tree homes for lunch.

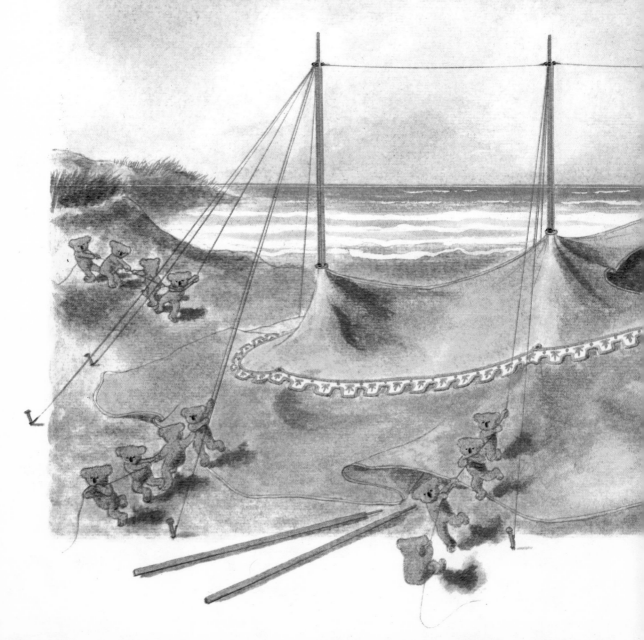

Real teddy bears are slow. It took them five years just to learn how to put up the circus tent. It took them even longer to get their acts ready and their circus clothes to fit right.

Seven years after being invited, the kangaroos were told it was time to come and see Bear Circus.

The program started with all the younger bears doing stunts. The act was first called BABY PARADE, but it took the bears so long to learn their tricks, they were almost grown up the day of the big opening.

The girl bears wore pink sashes and the boy bears wore blue sashes, and the name of the act was changed to

A CHILD'S GARDEN OF BEARS

Next came clowns. They were good, and the kangaroos thought they were funny, because kangaroos have pockets in their tummies.

The number they acted out is the first one all clowns learn when they go to clown school. It was performed by

THE THREE FUR BROTHERS

"Good morning, Farmer. I'll bet you can't balance a milk bottle on your forehead."
"I'll bet I can, Milkman."

"How does the sky look up there?"
"It's sunny and bright."

"It's raining down here."

"Hey, that's cheating!"

"I'm going to punch you in the nose."
"I've got a better idea."
"What is it?"

"Here comes the Banker. Why don't you play the trick on him?"
"Oh, good. I think I will."

"How's the sky up there?"
"Sunny and clear."

"It's raining down here."
"That's funny. I haven't felt a drop."

"I can't understand it. Are you wearing diapers?"

"No, a HOT-WATER BOTTLE!"

The Three Fur Brothers were followed by a magician

THE GREAT MYSTY BEAR

AND HIS PARTNER YOLANDA

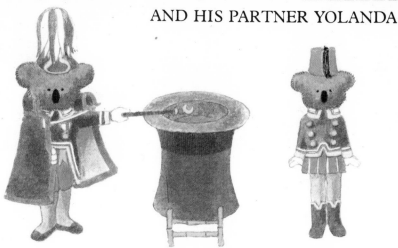

The Great Mysty Bear tapped on a top hat.

He showed the kangaroos that the top hat was empty.

He then pulled the flags of all nations from the top hat.

The Great Mysty Bear reached into the top hat

and pulled out a white bunny rabbit with a blue bow tie.

He then pulled out a fat carrot for the bunny rabbit.

Next on the program was a strong-bear act called

THE ALI BABAS

and featuring The Mighty Sindbad, carrying nine bears
four-bears high.

This was followed by the feature act of the evening, which had but one name:

SPLASHO!

The act started off rather simply with some teeter-board exercises. A bear would jump on one end of a see-saw, tossing the bear at the other end into a high somersault.

During this part of the act the incredible SPLASHO stood off to one side, wearing yellow tights and a bright orange cape.

Also, during this part of the act, three clowns were getting dressed at their dressing tables, which were set up at the farthest end of the big tent.

They dressed slowly, and when they were ready each clown took an umbrella with him.

Then one of them started pushing a bathtub, which was full of water and on wheels, toward the mat where SPLASHO was to perform.

When the three clowns started
walking, The Mighty Sindbad and
two of the heaviest bears, along with
two huge dumbbells, all climbed to
the top of a tall platform.

SPLASHO was now standing on
one end of the teeterboard. The
ringmaster removed his bright
orange cape.

The three clowns with the bathtub on wheels came slowly nearer.

At a signal from SPLASHO, The Mighty Sindbad, with the two heaviest bears on his back and a huge dumbbell in each hand, jumped down to the upper end of the teeterboard.

The three clowns with the bathtub on wheels edged ever closer.

The Mighty Sindbad, with heavy bears and dumbbells, came crashing down on the teeterboard, VARROOM!

Up went SPLASHO like a yellow streak.

The kangaroos gasped as he disappeared straight through the hole in the top of the tent, up into the sky outside. Then a great and frightening shout shot forth from the kangaroos. SPLASHO had gone up yellow; he came back GREEN!

The three clowns parked their bathtub on wheels and opened their umbrellas.

SPLASHO splashed down right in the middle of the three clowns' bathtub. There was a huge spray of water mixed with green things.

When SPLASHO stood up in his bathtub, he was no longer green, but he had an angry look on his face.

"They're back," he growled. "THE GRASSHOPPERS ARE BACK!"

All the bears and kangaroos rushed from the tent.

Once again the trees were bare and all the grass was gone.

"They've come back," growled the wise old bear. "The grasshoppers have come back and eaten all our food."

46

"How terrible," said the kangaroos, "but how lucky too, in a way. We're right here with you this time, so jump into our pockets or hang on to our necks. We'll hop off and soon find a new place. All aboard," they added.

The bears, in their circus clothes, took their places. They were off once again, thumping and bumping across the countryside. The kangaroos soon found more fine gum trees for the bears.

The bears hugged and kissed the kangaroos. Then the wise old bear said, "This is unfair. We were hoping to repay you with our circus for the first time you saved our lives. Now you've saved our lives again. It seems we'll never be able to repay you, never, never."

"We could never match your circus," said a kangaroo, "and besides, true friends never owe each other anything."

"Well, I must say that sounds sweet," said the wise old bear.

"Because it's true," said a kangaroo.

"I guess we are truly pals forever," said the wise old bear. "No more, no less."

"Pals forever!" echoed the kangaroos.

"What a happy way to end my first night at the circus," said a baby bear.

"Sleep well," said the kangaroos.